Dragon's Sledding Adventure

SCHOLASTIC READER · LEVEL 1 · 50-250 WORDS

Adapted by Becky Matheson
Based on an original TV episode written by Steve Westren

SCHOLASTIC INC.
New York   Toronto   London   Auckland
Sydney   Mexico City   New Delhi   Hong Kong

ISBN 978-0-545-20059-2

12 11 10 9 8 7 6 5 4 3 2 1   11 12 13 14 15 16/0

Printed in the U.S.A. 40
First printing, December 2011

It was a cold winter morning.
Dragon was in bed.

Dragon got out of bed.
He put on his warm hat and mittens.

He opened the door.
There was snow outside!

"I love snow!" said Dragon.

Dragon saw his friends.
They were going sledding.

Mailmouse used her mail bag
as a sled.

Ostrich used her float
as a sled.

Beaver used his trash can lid
as a sled.

Alligator used his snowboard
as a sled.

Dragon wanted to sled down the hill, too.

"I could use my broom," said Dragon.
But the broom was too small.

"I could use my sofa," Dragon said.
But the sofa was too big.

"I know!" said Dragon.
"I will use my rug as a sled."

But the rug got stuck
in the snow.

"Oh, no," said Dragon.
"I will never find a sled."

Then Dragon got hungry.
He ate pizza for lunch.

After lunch, Dragon washed the dishes.
Then he put the dishes away.

Dragon had a great idea!

"I could use my drawer as a sled," said Dragon.

Dragon pushed his drawer up the big hill.

Dragon sat in the drawer.

Then he slid down the hill.

Dragon had found the perfect sled!

He had a great day sledding
with his friends.
But it was very cold!

Dragon knew a great way
to end the cold day.

He invited everyone to his house for hot chocolate!

Now that everyone was warm,
Dragon got an idea!
"Let's go sledding again tomorrow!"
said Dragon.